Jeff LeVine
THE DAYS GO BY LIKE
BROKEN RECORDS

a No Hope collection
published by Slave Labor Graphics

Introduction
by Rob Neill

I was reading a magazine devoted to alternative (no quote marks please, that irony has left the building) music, when I came across this description of San Francisco in an article on lesbian mutilation fetishes and public bloodletting:

"The streets brim with bustling tops and bottoms and switches, butches, femmes and G-spot lesbians, masters, slaves, adult babies and PVC boy toys and the infinite combination thereof..."

Maybe. And a lot of people, even here, like to believe the stereotype of the Bay as, at worst, Sodom, or, at best, an amusement park. But there are relatively typical Americans living here. People who get by, live through the derision of their bosses, peers and (sometimes) their lovers, put in their eight to ten hours a day at their crummy job and try - in their spare time - to make some sense of it all and occasionally enjoy themselves.

Welcome to No Hope, lifestyles of the poor and bored.

Here, no one can afford to look like they live in a beer commercial. The upward mobility path is blocked by liars who tell you how tough it was for them. Support groups are limited to a few friends or (most of the time) yourself. And it is a 24-7 proposition that doesn't begin after "Seinfeld."

But it can also be a pretty glorious place. There are the aforementioned friends - and music, and beer. And someone - or the possibility of someone - who might not only like and sleep with you on a regular basis, but at least be no more crazy than you are.

That's not to say that Jeff isn't slightly nuts. Even I had trouble talking to him for awhile after reading "Velma." But these slim comics are a chronicle of the good - and shitty - aspects of being young, poor, smart and...hopeful.

Some people have a name for this group, "Generation X," and say it is about 80 million large. No, this is the "No Hope" generation. It's a lot smaller and its members' pressing worries are making rent and keeping the morons at the show from spilling their beer. And finding some peace.

And Jeff seems to find peace (he sure isn't finding much money) by using the dark to show us what's light. That's him in the bottom-right-hand panel of "Life Is," and he means it.

And if it is a struggle every day, why would they do it unless they had some hope?

Oh shit, I think I just gave the big joke away.

Rob Neill, Oakland, Calif., August 1995

No HopE

BY JEFF LEVINE · FOR MATURE READERS · $2.95 US $3.95 CAN

LIFE IS...

LIFE IS STINKY. SHIT- HOW AM I SUPPOSED TO KNOW? WHAT DAY IS IT?

LIFE IS NOT DISNEYLAND. I THINK IT IS WAKING UP EACH DAY AND DEALING WITH WHATEVER ISSUES YOU ARE FACING - GETTING THROUGH IT IN THE BEST POSSIBLE WAY. I WISH IT WAS DISNEYLAND.

LIFE IS PUSSY, MAN. PURE AND SIMPLE - PUSSY.

STILL A VIRGIN.

LIFE IS A TEST WE ALL FAIL. I THINK I SHOULD PROBABLY KILL MYSELF NOW AND AVOID THE WAIT.

ZZZ...ZZZ...

LIFE IS SHOPPING.

LIFE IS HATE. 100% PURE FUCKING HATE!

LIFE IS NINTENDO! YEAH!

LIFE IS (PLEASE DON'T LAUGH) DOING YOUR BEST TO MAKE OTHER PEOPLE FEEL GOOD.

THE GREAT EXPERIMENT OR A DANGEROUS IDEA

TODAY WAS A PRETTY IMPORTANT DAY.

WE DID SOMETHING THAT IS GOING TO CHANGE MY LIFE FOREVER.

IT WAS SO MAJOR THAT MY ROOMMATES AND I HAD TO DEBATE IT FOR THE LAST SIX MONTHS.

TODAY WE CANCELED OUR CABLE SERVICE.

I'M NOT SURE IF WE MADE THE CORRECT DECISION.

RIGHT NOW KNOWING I CAN'T GO TURN ON THE TV AND FLIP THROUGH 100 CHANNELS IS ACTUALLY CAUSEING ME PHYSICAL PAIN.

MY ROOMMATE MIP IS SITTING ON THE COUCH STILL IN SHOCK.

WHERE'S THE REMOTE JEFF?!

WHAT AM I GOING TO DO NOW? I'M SO SCARED!

BAH!

LIVING IN DOWNTOWN SAN JOSE NO CABLE MEANS NO TV.

WE CAN ONLY KIND OF PICK UP ONE CHANNEL OF TV, BUT I THINK THAT ONE IS PBS.

NOT THAT THERE WAS EVER ANYTHING GOOD ON CABLE - THAT'S WHY WE HAD IT DISCONNECTED.

BUT STILL, WE DID MANAGE TO SPEND MOST OF OUR FREE TIME WATCHING IT.

NOW I DON'T KNOW WHAT I'LL DO WITH ALL THAT EXTRA TIME. I MAY EVEN HAVE TO GO OUTSIDE INTO THE REAL WORLD FOR ENTERTAINMENT!

GOD - PLEASE GIVE ME THE STRENGTH TO SURVIVE.

PART TWO
THE NEXT DAY THE TRUTH DAWNs FOR BUTTHEAD

PART THREE DAY THREE THE CONVERSATION

PART FOUR — THE LECTURE

FOR TOO LONG WE HAVE ALLOWED OUR LIVES TO BE CONTROLLED BY TV.

THEY HOOKED US WHEN WE WERE YOUNG.

GODDAMN IT - THAT SHIT WASN'T FAIR.

WE DIDN'T KNOW BETTER WE DIDN'T KNOW WHAT ALL THAT TV WOULD END UP DOING TO OUR BRAINS.

IT'S INCREDIBLE HOW THEY CAN FILL UP SO MANY HOURS WITH COMPLETELY MINDLESS PAP.

THE SHEER QUANTITY OF IT ALL IS OVERPOWERING.

BUT DON'T BE FOOLED.

TRUST ME - IF YOU HAVEN'T SEEN EVERY EPISODE OF THREE'S COMPANY YOU AREN'T MISSING ANYTHING.

IT'S ALL CRAP.

DESIGNED FOR THE LOWEST COMMON DENOMINATOR.

IT REALLY DOES ROT YOUR BRAINS. NNNN...

THERE REALLY IS A LOT BETTER STUFF WE CAN DO.

IT'S TIME FOR US TO GET UP OFF OUR BUTTS AND SIEZE CONTROL OF OUR LIVES.

NO MORE CHEERS. NO MORE COSBY. NO MORE OF THAT FUCKING ERKEL KID! NO MORE NIGHT COURT. NO MORE OF THAT 90210 BULLSHIT. FUCK 60 MINUTES!

GO OUTSIDE. READ A BOOK. WRITE A BOOK. DRAW A COMIC. WHATEVER! FOLLOW YOUR DREAMS - MAKE YOUR OWN MYTHS.

KILL YOUR TELEVISION!

PART SIX
THREE WEEKS LATER
I THINK I'VE FINALLY DONE IT. I'VE KICKED MY TV HABIT, BUT THE WITHDRAWALS WERE A BITCH.
LIFE REALLY IS A LOT BETTER NOW. I'VE BEEN SPENDING A LOT MORE TIME THINKING, READING AND GOING OUT AND LIVING LIFE TO THE FULLEST.
I THINK IT'S EVEN HELPING MY COMICS. MY HEAD IS SO MUCH CLEARER- GOOD IDEAS KEEP POPPING OUT AT AN INCREDIBLE RATE, AND I'VE BEEN GETTING A LOT MORE GOOD WORK DONE.
ALL I CAN SAY IS THAT A MONTH AND A HALF AGO WHEN I USED TO WATCH TV ALL THE TIME I WAS ALWAYS MISERABLE. NOW I'M ALMOST ALWAYS IN A GREAT MOOD.
SOMETIMES MY ROOMMATES AND I EVEN TALK NOW - AND IT'S NOT THAT BAD.

DROWNING
IN A SEA OF BOREDOM

SHIT!

ZZZZ...

I DON'T BELIEVE THIS! HOW DID MY LIFE END UP TURNING OUT SO FUCKED UP? I'M STUCK IN A SHITTY JOB - NINE TO FIVE - GOING NOWHERE - BARELY MAKING ENOUGH MONEY TO PAY RENT AND BUY A LITTLE FOOD NOW AND THEN. MY BOY-FRIEND IS A TOTAL FUCKING LOSER WHO IS PRACTICALLY IMPOTENT...

ZZZ...

I DON'T THINK I'VE EVER BEEN THIS BORED BEFORE IN MY ENTIRE LIFE.

WHEN I WAS A KID I COULDN'T WAIT TO FUCKING GROW UP. I THOUGHT LIFE AS AN ADULT WOULD BE EX-CITING... A FUN FILLED WONDERLAND.

SNORT

NOW THAT I AM FINALLY AN "ADULT," I WISH I COULD BE A LITTLE KID AGAIN. LIFE AS AN ADULT SUCK SHIT - PLAIN AND SIMPLE.

ZZZZ...

GODDAMN! I AM SO FUCKING BORED AS FUCK!

LUNCHBREAK

JL 7.23.92 THE END

ANOTHER FRIDAY NIGHT

YOU KNOW, I SAW THE STRANGEST THING ON T.V. TODAY. I WAS WATCHING THAT SALLY JESSE RAPHEAL THING... YOU KNOW WHAT I'M TALKING ABOUT?

NO.

THAT TALK SHOW WITH THE BLOND LADY WITH THE FUNNY RED GLASSES?

I'VE NEVER SEEN IT.

ANYWAY, SHE WAS DOING THIS SHOW ABOUT PEOPLE WHO HAD WEIRD TYPES OF CANCER, OR SOME KIND OF DISEASE THAT LEFT THEM DEFORMED.

SO, HER SECOND GUEST WAS THIS STRANGE LOOKING OLD MAN WHO WAS TELLING THE STORY OF ALL HIS SURGERIES AND STUFF. THERE WAS SOMETHING REALLY WEIRD ABOUT THE WAY HIS FACE LOOKED, BUT I COULDN'T FIGURE OUT EXACTLY WHAT. FINALLY HE GOT NEAR TO THE END OF HIS STORY AND SALLY ASKED HIM, "SO WHAT DID THEY END UP DOING TO YOUR NOSE.."

AND HE SAID, "BECAUSE OF IT BEING SO FILLED WITH CANCER THEY CUT IT OFF." AND THEN HE TOOK OFF HIS GLASSES AND HIS NOSE WAS JUST A FAKE THING ATTATCHED TO THEM! HE JUST HAD A BIG HOLE IN THE MIDDLE OF HIS FACE... IT WAS THE WEIRDEST THING I'VE EVER SEEN ON T.V. THEN HE STARTED TO CRY.

SHIT!

BUT SHE WAS TWENTY THREE - CAN HER PARENTS DO THAT?

IF YOU HAVE AS MUCH MONEY AS THEY DO YOU CAN DO ANYTHING.

AT FIRST I WAS PISSED, BUT IT'S BEEN THREE DAYS AND I'VE HONESTLY BEEN FEELING A LOT BETTER NOW THAT SHE IS FINALLY OUT OF MY HAIR. I JUST DECIDED IT WOULD BE BEST IF WE NEVER SEE EACH OTHER AGAIN.

YOU BASTARD! HOW C YOU JUST ABANDON HER

KATHY - LET'S DANCE. OKAY?

OKAY... BUT FIRST I GOTTA CHECK MY COAT. IT'S GETTING HOT IN HERE.

FINE.

YOU'RE KILLING ME YOU FUCK

LOOK! THE PEOPLE OUT THERE IN THE AUDIENCE. THE LADY THERE WITH THE LONG EARS - THEY'RE GETTIN' LONGER.

AND THE GUY BACK THERE WITH THE CUTE TOMATO - HE'S GETTING ALL FUZZY.

YEAH, THEY'VE GOT IT. EVERYBODY OUT THERE'S GOT RABBITITIS!!! AAAAAGGHHH!

HEY DOUG, WHAT'S UP?

NOT MUCH. I'M JUST WATCHING CARTOONS. WHERE HAVE YOU BEEN?

I JUST PICKED UP SOMETHING NEW THAT I KNOW YOU'RE REALLY GOING TO LIKE. CHECK THIS OUT!

TA DA!

DON'T FORGET HER WALLET, WE NEED MONEY FOR BEER LATER.

BOB VS. THE SUN

IT'S SUCH A NICE DAY OUT TODAY THAT BETTY AND I'VE DECIDED TO GO FOR A WALK UP TO THE PARK. WE MADE UP SOME SANDWICHES AND WANT YOU TO COME.

THANKS, BUT NO THANKS.

COME ON BOB - YOU NEVER GO OUT OF THE HOUSE ANYMORE, AND WE'RE GETTING WORRIED ABOUT YOU!

I JUST DON'T LIKE IT OUT THERE! I'VE GOT EVERYTHING I NEED IN HERE.

REALLY BOB - IT WILL DO YOU GOOD TO GET SOME SUN. YOU'VE BEEN LOOKING AWFULLY PALE LATELY.

GAG! I FUCKING HATE THE SUN!

WHAT! THE SUN IS NICE, ESPECIALLY TODAY. WHAT DO YOU THINK YOU ARE, SOME KIND OF VAMPIRE?

NO NO! NOT AT ALL! WHAT WOULD MAKE YOU THINK THAT? IT'S JUST THAT THE SUN IS REALLY BAD FOR YOU - ESPECIALLY NOW WITH ALL THE HOLES IN THE OZONE LAYER. THE ULTRAVIOLET RAYS FROM THE SUN GIVE YOU CATARACTS WHICH COULD LEAD TO BLINDNESS, AND THE RADIATION CAN CAUSE YOUR DNA TO MUTATE SO YOU GET SKIN CANCER. YOU CAN EVEN GET MELANOMA FROM THE SUN, WHICH IS OFTEN FATAL! THERE'S NO WAY I'M GOING OUTSIDE. FORGET IT!

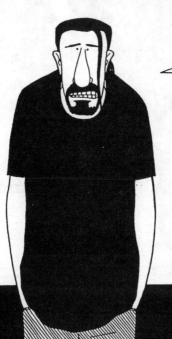

MY TRAIN STORY

I RECENTLY TOOK THE ANTRAK TRAIN FROM SAN JOSE TO LOS ANGELES.

IT WAS A FAIRLY UN-EVENTFUL TRIP EX-CEPT FOR ONE ODD INSTANCE.

I WENT DOWNSTAIRS TO TAKE A PISS IN THE BATHROOM AND WAS GREETED WITH AN AMAZING SIGHT (NOT TO MENTION AN AMAZING SMELL)!

INSIDE WAS THE MOST MAMMOTH SHIT I HAD EVER SEEN!

IT WAS JUST SITTING THERE. I FLUSHED THE TOILET, BUT IT WOULDN'T GO DOWN.

SWOOSH

I HAD NO CHOICE SO I RELIEVED MYSELF RIGHT ON IT, AND WHEN I FLUSHED AGAIN IT JUST STAY-ED STUCK THERE.

LUCKILY WHEN I GOT OUT OF THE BATHROOM NOBODY WAS AROUND SO THEY WOULDN'T THINK I HAD DONE IT.

I WONDER IF IT IS STILL THERE?

THE END YES IT'S TRUE

WEDNESDAY

RALPH

LOOK AT ALL YOU PEOPLE HERE RIDING THIS BUS! YOU'RE ALL SUCH FOOLS!

EVERYDAY GOING TO WORK TO YOUR NICE SAFE JOBS - AFRAID TO LIVE!

YOU'RE SUCH SHEEP, AND YOU'RE CONTENT!

DON'T YOU KNOW THE WORLD IS GOING TO FUCKING END IN ELEVEN MORE DAYS!

YOU THINK I'M CRAZY, BUT I KNOW I'M NOT.

I KNOW WHAT THE FUCK I'M TALKING ABOUT! THE WORLD IS GOING TO FUCKING END!

ALL OF YOU ARE THE ONES WHO ARE CRAZY! YOU'RE ALL WORSE THAN CRAZY...

YOU'RE HAPPY.

SNIF

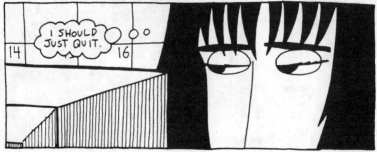

PLEASE KATHY - DON'T START GETTING HOSTILE.
I DON'T WANT TO FIGHT.
CAN'T YOU JUST STAY HOME THIS ONE NIGHT FOR ME! WE COULD SPEND SOME TIME ALONE - JUST THE TWO OF US FOR A CHANGE.

WE'VE JUST SPENT THE LAST HOUR TOGETHER HONEY. ISN'T THAT ENOUGH? SOMETIMES YOU ARE SO POSSESSIVE.

OKAY OKAY. YOU WIN. CAN YOU JUST GIVE ME A RIDE HOME?

NOW YOU'RE ANGRY. I DIDN'T WANT YOU TO GET ANGRY.

JOHN - I'M NOT ANGRY... COULD YOU PLEASE JUST GIVE ME A RIDE HOME?

VROOM

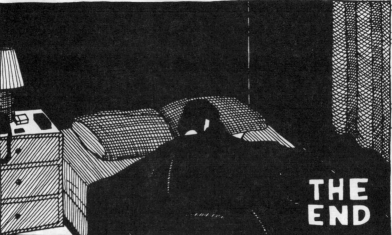

THE
END

HATE MY LIFE

ZzZzz...

UHHHG.

OH SHIT...

OH SHIT. OH SHIT. OH SHIT.
OW... OW... OW... MY HEAD.

ACK! WHAT TIME IS IT? SHIT.

GOTTA GET UP AND GET TO WORK. NO... I WAS
FIRED AGAIN... SHIT. I DRANK WAY TOO FUCK-
ING MUCH LAST NIGHT. WHAT WAS I THINKING?
MAN, MY HEAD HURTS. MAYBE I SHOULD JUST STAY
HERE IN BED.

DAMN IT! I DON'T BELIEVE YOU DANIEL - FIRED AGAIN! WHAT IS THIS NOW... THE FIFTH JOB YOU'VE ALREADY LOST THIS YEAR... AND IT'S ONLY MARCH!

WHEN ARE YOU GOING TO GROW UP AND TAKE A LITTLE RESPONSIBILITY FOR YOUR OWN LIFE!

AND WHILE I'M HERE LET ME ADD THAT YOUR MOTHER AND I DIDN'T APPRECIATE YOU STUBLING IN DRUNK AT FOUR IN THE MORNING!

WE COULD HARDLY SLEEP THROUGH THE SOUNDS OF YOUR THROWING UP IN THE BATHROOM. YOU HAVE NO RESPECT FOR US!

OH... THAT'S WHAT THAT FUNNY TASTE IN MY MOUTH WAS.

THE LEAST YOU COULD HAVE DONE WAS CLEAN UP AFTER YOURSELF!

DO YOU THINK YOU GUYS COULD GIVE ME A BREAK RIGHT NOW... HUH? I FEEL LIKE HELL.

YEAH... I'D LIKE TO GIVE YOU A BREAK! THAT'S WHAT YOU GET FOR BEING IRRESPONSIBLE

JUST THINK ABOUT THIS... WE'RE NOT GOING TO LET YOU LIVE HERE AND TAKE ADVANTAGE OF US FOREVER IF THIS IS THE WAY YOU'RE GOING TO CONTINUE TO BEHAVE!

YOU'RE IN DEEP SHIT, YOUNG MAN.

INTRODUCING A NEW No Hope REGULAR FEATURE
JOHNNY BORED'S TALK SHOW REPORT

INTERMISSION

HI!

I HAD THE WEIRDEST DREAM LAST NIGHT.

I'M POSITIVE IT WOULD MAKE MY WEIRDEST COMIC YET...

THE ONLY PROBLEM IS THAT I CAN'T REMEMBER IT AT ALL.

I CAN NEVER REMEMBER MY DREAMS- IT REALLY SUCKS.

IF ONLY I COULD REMEMBER MY DREAMS I COULD MAKE SOME **REALLY ORIGINAL COMICS**...

MY FAMILY STILL THINKS THAT DRAWING THESE "WEIRD" COMICS AND DOING ALL THESE SMALL PRESS THINGS THAT MAKE NO MONEY IS JUST A PHASE FOR ME.

THEY FIGURE THAT SOMEDAY I'LL MEET THE RIGHT GIRL AND SHE'LL BRING ME TO MY SENSES.

I'LL SETTLE DOWN WITH HER, MAYBE HAVE A FEW KIDS, AND GIVE ALL THIS CRAP UP.

MAYBE I'LL BE ABLE TO GET A JOB AT A GOOD COMPANY LIKE MARVEL, DRAWING SPIDERMAN, AND MAKE LOTS OF MONEY - THEY PRAY.

"IT WOULD BE SO NICE IF YOU WOULD DRAW A COMIC I COULD SHOW TO MY FRIENDS," HINTS MY MOM.

SOMETIMES I WISH THEY WERE RIGHT, BUT I **KNOW** THEY AREN'T...

YUP...I'M DOOMED.

END

NO BULLSHIT EVER

LAST NIGHT I WAS HANGING OUT IN THE PARK WITH FIVE OF MY FRIENDS AT ABOUT TWO-THIRTY IN THE MORNING.

A WHOLE SQUAD OF COPS CAME AND STARTED TRYING TO BEAT THE SHIT OUTTA US AND REMOVE US FROM THE PUBLIC PARK.

NEXT THING I KNEW, PRESIDENT CLINTON WAS THERE AND I STARTED YELLING SHIT AT HIM ABOUT HIS FASCIST USE OF THE MILITARY IN SOMALIA AND IRAQ, AND HIS HEALTH CARE PLAN.

SUDDENLY ONE OF THE COPS WENT DOWN AND IN THE CONFUSION I ESCAPED, ALONG WITH ALL MY FRIENDS.

WE RE-GROUPED AT A FRIENDLY LITTLE HOTEL WE KNOW, CLEANED UP OUR WOUNDS AND CAUGHT SOME Z'S.

IN THE MORNING I WAS HEADING OUT TO GET SOME COFFEE WHEN MY FRIEND CAME RUNNING UP WITH THE NEWSPAPER.
LOOK!!!

ON THE FRONT PAGE WAS AN ACCOUNT OF OUR BATTLE WITH THE POLICE, BUT THEY BLAMED US FOR THE DEAD COP (WHICH ISN'T TRUE... HE WAS KILLED BY **FRIENDLY** FIRE FROM ONE OF HIS FELLOW COPS).

HOWEVER, THE PART OF THE NEWSPAPER REPORT THAT WAS REALLY DISTURBING WAS THAT THEY SAID I HAD BEEN KILLED IN THE BATTLE TOO!
DOOM DOOM
FEATURES PAGE
LEARNS NEW TRICKS
GAA!!!

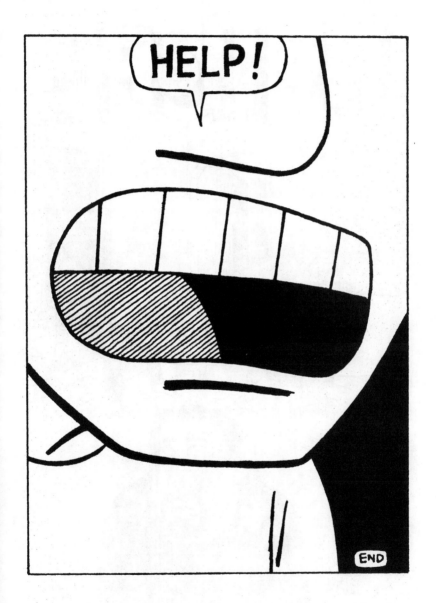

Happy Comic Version 3.0

JOHN'S JOB HUNT

I GUESS A GOOD PLACE TO START WOULD BE LOOKING THROUGH THE CLASSIFIED ADS IN THE NEWSPAPER.

YEAH... I CAN GO BUY THE PAPER AND THEN GO UP TO THE DONUT SHOP AND HAVE A CUP OF COFFEE AND A COUPLE OF DONUTS SO I'LL HAVE A LOT OF ENERGY!

YEAH! WHAT I'M GOING TO DO IS MAKE THIS WHOLE JOB THING INTO AN ADVENTURE! IT'LL BE FUN!!!

HEY JOHN!

DANA! HI!

WHAT'S UP?

YOU'RE NOT GOING TO BELIEVE THIS BUT I'M LOOKING FOR A JOB! I DECIDED THAT NO MATTER WHAT, I'M GOING TO GET A JOB TODAY! I'M JUST SO SICK OF BEING UNEMPLOYED AND I REALLY NEED SOME MONEY BAD.

YEAH-I KNOW WHAT YOU MEAN! THAT'S COOL... GOT ANY GOOD LEADS?

I DON'T KNOW... I'VE CIRCLED A FEW THINGS, BUT NOTHING TERRIBLY EXCITING. MOSTLY TELE-MARKETING... AND ONE DISHWASHER.

YUCK.

I KNOW, THEY ALL SUCK... BUT I'M NOT QUALIFIED FOR ANY GOOD JOBS... I'M NOT REALLY QUALIFIED FOR ANYTHING. FUCK I HATE LIFE.

DO YOU WANNA JUST BUY SOME BEER AND COME OVER TO MY PLACE? I'VE GOT SOME POT TOO.

NO... I'M REALLY SERIOUS ABOUT GETTING A JOB TODAY. MY LIFE IS SO FUCKED UP. I'VE GOTTA GET RESPONSIBLE.

WHAT KIND OF POT?

IT'S PRETTY GOOD.

OKAY, LET'S GO!

... AND THEY'RE ALL ALMOST EXACTLY THE SAME! YOU JUST WANDER AROUND KILLING THINGS! THE GRAPHICS MIGHT NOT HAVE BEEN AS GOOD ON THE OLD GAMES, BUT MOST OF THEM WERE A FUCK OF A LOT MORE INVENTIVE. GAMES LIKE GALAGA, Q-BERT, TEMPEST, CENTIPEDE AND TRON... THEY WERE JUST SO MUCH MORE FUN THAN THE STUPID GAMES THEY HAVE OUT NOW... LIKE STREETFICHTER SUPER DUPER CHAMPIONSHIP. ALL YOU GET TO DO IS PUNCH SOMEBODY UNTIL THEY FALL OVER! I JUST CAN'T UNDERSTAND WHY IT'S SO POPULAR.

HAVE YOU GUYS HEARD ABOUT THE STAR TREK THE NEXT GENERATION VIRTUAL REALITY GAME THEY'RE PUTTING OUT?

SPEAKING OF STAR TREK THE NEXT GENERATION... I JUST SAW THE MOST ANNOYING EPISODE EVER!

OKAY, HERE'S THE STORY... PICARD, GUINAN, ENSIGN RO, AND KEIKO ARE FLYING IN A SHUTTLE CRAFT THAT IS DESTROYED BY SOME WEIRD SPACE ANOMALY.

LUCKILY THEY ARE TRANSPORTED BACK TO THE ENTERPRISE JUST IN TIME, BUT SOMETHING WENT WRONG AND ALL FOUR OF THEM HAVE TRANSFORMED BACK INTO TEN YEAR OLDS (ALTHOUGH THEY STILL HAVE ALL THEIR ADULT MEMORIES AND INTELLIGENCE).

IN THE END THOUGH IT TURNS OUT TO BE A BLESSING BECAUSE THEY SAVE THE SHIP FROM A RENEGADE FERENGI TAKE-OVER!

DR. CRUSHER FINDS OUT THAT WHAT HAPPENED WAS A TRANSPORTER ACCIDENT THAT REMOVED A SPECIFIC PART OF THEIR DNA, TURNING THEM BACK INTO TEN YEAR OLDS; HOWEVER, THEY WILL CONTINUE TO AGE AGAIN NATURALLY.

SHE GETS EVERYBODY TO GO BACK THROUGH THE TRANSPORTER, RE-INSERTS THE MISSING DNA STRAND FROM OLD TRANSPORTER RECORDS AND PICARD AND ALL RETURN TO THEIR NATURAL AGES. FADE TO CREDITS.

HOLD IT A SECOND! IT SEEMS LIKE SOMEBODY FORGOT TO MENTION THAT THEY NOW KNOW THE SECRET TO ETERNAL LIFE... NOT TO MENTION ETERNAL YOUTH!!!

ANYTIME ANYBODY WANTS TO, THEY SHOULD BE ABLE TO STEP INTO A TRANSPORTER AND BE TURNED BACK INTO A TEN YEAR OLD WITH ALL THEIR LIFE EXPERIENCE ENTACT.

SOMEHOW THOUGH, THAT APPLICATION OF THEIR TECHNOLOGY DOESN'T SEEM TO BE OF INTEREST TO THE CREW OF THE ENTERPRISE! THEY SEEM TO BE SAYING, "OH YEAH... ETERNAL LIFE, WHO CARES."

I FUCKING CARE!!!

ETERNAL LIFE WOULD BE SO COOL! GETTING OLD AND DYING ARE THE MOST FUCKED UP THINGS ABOUT LIFE.

I WANT TO LIVE FOREVER, NOT JUST GO TO TEN-FORWARD TO GET ANOTHER DRINK.

TO BE TEN YEARS OLD, BUT NOT A STUPID MORON... THAT WOULD BE HEAVEN!

COULD IT BE THAT SOMEHOW THEY JUST DIDN'T NOTICE THEY HAD DISCOVERED THE SECRET TO ETERNAL LIFE. NO... THEY CAN'T BE THAT DUMB! I WONDER IF THIS IS SOME KIND OF CONSPIRACY.

YOU'RE SO FUCKING STONED JOHN!

YEAH...

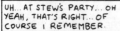

END

FUNNY STORY

WANNA HEAR A FUNNY STORY?

WELL, YOU KNOW HOW RIGHT NOW I'M LIVING WITH MY GRANDMA, BECAUSE I'M DOWN IN LOS ANGELES WORKING MY SHITTY JOB FOR THREE WEEKS SO I CAN MAKE SOME MONEY SO I CAN AFFORD TO MAKE SHITTY COMICS LIKE THIS...

ANYWAY, LAST NIGHT WHEN I WAS LAYING IN BED TRYING TO FALL ASLEEP...

HONK

HONK

HONK

THERE WAS THIS LOUD NOISE COMING THROUGH MY WALL THAT WAS KEEPING ME AWAKE. I THOUGHT IT WAS SOMEBODY PRACTICING THE TUBA!

HONK

I WAS GETTING PRETTY ANNOYED BECAUSE IT WAS KEEPING ME AWAKE. I COULDN'T FIGURE OUT WHAT KIND OF FUCKING ASSHOLE WOULD BE PLAYING THE TUBA AT 12:20.

HONK

SHIT!

WHEN I FINALLY FIGURED OUT THAT IT WAS MY GRANDMA SNORING I COULDN'T STOP LAUGHING! HA HA HA!

THE END OF ANOTHER TRUE STORY

IT'S REALLY NOT AS BAD AS IT LOOKS

WISH I WAS DEAD

For the Love of Velma

THE U.S.A. CABLE CHANNEL IS SUCH A BITCH!

I MEAN, I USED TO BE A FAIRLY NORMAL PERSON. I HAD A JOB, A CAR, AND A GIRLFRIEND. I WAS PLAYING THE GAME ACCORDING TO THE RULES.

THEN I GOT CABLE TV.

I WAS FLIPPING THROUGH THE CHANNELS ONE EVENING AFTER WORK AND CAME ACROSS AN OLD EPISODE OF SCOOBY DOO THAT THE U.S.A. CHANNEL WAS RE-RUNNING.

WHEN THE CHARACTER VELMA CAME ON I WAS SUDDENLY OVERCOME WITH DESIRE.

MY DICK HARDENED INTO A MIGHTY CONCRETE PILLAR.

I TOOK OFF MY SOCK AND STARTED MASTURBATING RIGHT INTO IT. IN SECONDS I CAME IN A HUGE BURST LIKE NEVER BEFORE.

GAH!

WHAT IS REALLY HORRIBLE WAS THAT I COULDN'T STOP. FOR SOME REASON MASTUR- BATING INTO OLD SOCKS TO THE CARTOON IMAGE OF VELMA WAS THE BEST SEX I'D EVER HAD.

NOW I'VE LOST MY JOB, MY GIRLFRIEND LEFT ME, AND I SOLD MY CAR TO PAY FOR MY CABLE BILL AND TO BUY A HUGE ASSORT- MENT OF MEN'S SOCKS.

THE GOOD NEWS IS NOW THAT I'M ALWAYS HOME I HAVE TIME TO WATCH SCOOBY DOO ALL THREE TIMES THE U.S.A. CHANNEL AIRS IT EVERY DAY.

I LOVE YOU VELMA!

END.

A SCARY STORY

Written by Jason LeVine   Drawn by Jeff LeVine

STARRING THE BERRY BROTHERS
IDENTICAL TWIN ALBINOS FROM CLEVELAND

IT ALL BEGAN ONE FINE DAY IN OCTOBER. NIGEL WAS SITTING ON THE COUCH READING A CEREAL BOX WHEN HIS BROTHER TERRY BURST INTO THE ROOM. THERE WAS AN AGITATED LOOK ON HIS FACE.

NIGEL! THANK GOODNESS YOU'RE HERE!

WHAT IS IT TERRY? YOU HAVE AN AGITATED LOOK ON YOUR FACE.

I'M IN TERRIBLE TROUBLE! YOU WOULDN'T HAPPEN TO HAVE 250 DOLLARS I COULD BORROW, WOULD YOU? I NEED IT BAD, REAL BAD.

NIGEL PULLS OUT HIS WALLET AND LOOKS.

WELL, LET'S SEE... I'VE GOT... FORTY SEVEN CENTS.

THAT WON'T DO. YOU SEE, I OWE A GUY NAMED ROCCO 250 DOLLARS, AND I PROMISED I WOULD PAY HIM BY TOMORROW, BUT NOW... I DON'T KNOW WHAT TO DO. I'M SO AFRAID!!!

GOT MY TWO-FIFTY TERRY, OR DO I HAVE TO DISLOCATE YOUR ARMS? HA! HA!

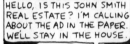

IT DOESN'T LOOK TOO SCARY, DOES IT NIGEL?

NO, NOT AT ALL.

GULP!

SUDDENLY THE FRONT DOOR OPENS REVEALING A HIDEOUS HUNCHBACK!

GOOD EVENING. WE'VE BEEN EXPECTING YOU. COME IN... MY NAME IS BOBO. I'LL SHOW YOU TO YOUR ROOM.

WHAT IS IT EXACTLY THAT WE HAVE TO DO?

PEOPLE SAY THIS HOUSE IS HAUNTED AND WE WANT YOU TO PROVE THAT IT ISN'T. ALL YOU HAVE TO DO IS STAY HERE FOR ONE NIGHT, AND COME TOMORROW MORNING (IF YOU'RE STILL ALIVE) YOU MAY GO - 250 DOLLARS RICHER. IT'S EASY MONEY!

OH PLEASE GOD...

THIS IS YOUR ROOM...YOU TWO CAN SLEEP HERE. THERE'S NOTHING TO BE AFRAID OF. TRY TO GET SOME REST AND HAVE A NICE NIGHT.

YOU HUNGRY, NIGEL? I SURE AM. OH, LOOK...HERE'S A REFRIGERATOR.

WHAT DID I DO TO DESERVE THIS LORD?

HE OPENS THE REFRIGERATOR ONLY TO FIND — — —

GOOD HEAVENS!

NIGEL, YOU'RE NOT GOING TO BELIEVE THIS, BUT I'M IN THE REFRIGERATOR!!!

WHAT? THAT'S IMPOSSIBLE!

TERRY OPENS THE REFRIGERATOR FOR HIS BROTHER, BUT THE BODY IS NO LONGER THERE!

IT'S VANISHED!

LOOK, MAYBE WE SHOULD TRY TO GET SOME SLEEP LIKE THAT GUY SAID.

I DON'T THINK I COULD SLEEP IN THIS PLACE. IT GIVES ME THE CREEPS!!!

FIVE MINUTES LATER...

ZZZZZ ZZZZZ

ZZZZZ ZZZZZ

A FEW HOURS PASS. SUDDENLY TERRY WAKES UP AND MAKES A TERRIFYING DIS- COVERY — IT APPEARS THAT NIGEL HAS DISAPPEARED!

OH NO! WHAT AM I GOING TO DO? IT'S ALL MY FAULT.. I GUESS I'LL HAVE TO GO FIND HIM. **THAT FOOL!**

HE LOOKS OUT THE DOOR AND SEES A STRANGE SIGHT — THE HUNCHBACK HAS REVEALED A SINISTER TRAP- DOOR AND IS CREEPING DOWN IT, LAUGHING LIKE A VERITABLE FIEND.

HA HA HA!

MUSTERING HIS COURAGE, TERRY FOLLOWS THE QUEER APPARITION DOWN INTO THE STYGIAN BOWELS OF THE CASTLE.

TIPTOE TIPTOE

HEE HEE

Greetings Loser

a Short Walk Later

* that's sarcasm you moron.

the next day

END

"LADIES AND GENTLEMEN MEET MR. SUN"

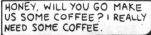

HONEY, WILL YOU GO MAKE US SOME COFFEE? I REALLY NEED SOME COFFEE.

WHY DON'T YOU GIVE RICHARD A CALL AND SEE IF HE'LL DRIVE US TO THE BEACH?

WHAT? WHY THE HELL DO YOU WANT HIM TO COME? THAT DOESN'T SOUND VERY ROMANTIC!

...NOR DOES TAKING THE BUS TO THE BEACH.

...IF YOU HADN'T SOLD YOUR MOTORCYCLE...

OKAY, I'LL CALL HIM! WHY DON'T YOU GO MAKE THAT COFFEE, KATHY?

SURE!

HEY RICHARD, WHAT'S UP MAN? I DIDN'T WAKE YOU UP DID I? OH SHIT... I'M SORRY.

ANYWAY MAN, YOU SHOULD BE UP BY NOW. YOU DON'T HAVE TO DO ANYTHING TODAY, DO YOU? GREAT! GET UP AND GET OVER HERE. WE'RE GOING TO THE BEACH AND YOU'RE DRIVING!

TO BE CONTINUED...

"LADIES AND GENTLEMEN MEET MR. SUN" PART 2

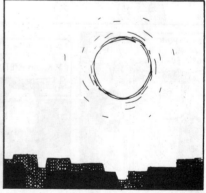

SUDDENLY A GIANT METEORITE STREAKED THROUGH THE SKY OVER THE CITY. IT CRASHED TO EARTH DIRECTLY ON TOP OF OUR HEROES CAR...KILLING THEM ALL PRACTICALLY INSTANTLY.

...and you think your life sucks now.

DO YOU EVER THINK ABOUT GROWING OLD?

...AND HAVING YOUR WHOLE BODY HURT ALL THE TIME...

...AND BEING SLOW... NOT BEING ABLE TO RUN OR JUMP OR EVEN STAY STANDING UP ON A BUS.

RECENTLY I'VE BEEN THINKING A LOT ABOUT GROWING OLD... AND WHEN I DO, I GET SCARED.

I DON'T KNOW... I GUESS I'VE MET A FEW COOL OLD PEOPLE.

...BUT MOST OF THE OLD PEOPLE I'VE EVER SEEN ARE JUST THE MOST HORRIBLE, MISERABLE THINGS WALKING THE EARTH.

THEY SEEM TO JUST BE WAITING TO DIE.

I KNOW I DON'T WANT TO END UP LIKE THAT!

Nothin' TO DO

BAD LUCK BOY

a close call

I'D JUST SPENT A NICE AFTERNOON KILLING TIME AT THE LIBRARY AND WAS WALKING HOME AND THINKING ABOUT EATING SOME ICE CREAM.

AS I WAS HEADING UP THE DRIVEWAY TO MY APARTMENT I NOTICED A STRANGE LOOKING GUY SITTING DOWN ON MY NEIGHBOR'S FRONT STEP, BUT I REALLY DIDN'T THINK MUCH ABOUT IT.

WHEN I STEPPED INTO MY HOUSE I SAW SOMEBODY I DIDN'T RECOGNIZE HUNCHED OVER MY ROOMMATES NINTENDO.

HE LOOKED UP AT ME WITH A STRANGE EXPRESSION. I SAID...

HELLO.

SUDDENLY I REALIZED THAT HE'D BROKEN INTO MY HOUSE AND WAS IN THE PROCESS OF STEALING OUR VIDEO GAME SYSTEM!!!

I POINTED AT HIM...THEN POINTED OUT THE FRONT DOOR.

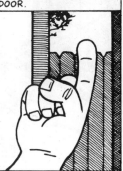

HE STOOD UP AND SAID...

SORRY.

HE WALKED OUT THE DOOR AND HEADED DOWN THE DRIVEWAY. THE STRANGE GUY WHO WAS SITTING ON MY NEIGHBORS STEP JOINED HIM, AND THEY DISAPPEARED AROUND THE CORNER.

I WENT BACK INTO MY APARTMENT AND CHECKED TO MAKE SURE THEY HADN'T TAKEN ANY THING. I GUESS I GOT HOME JUST IN TIME BECAUSE EVERYTHING WAS STILL THERE. I GUESS I WAS PRETTY LUCKY TOO THAT THEY DIDN'T HAVE A GUN OR ANYTHING, AND LEFT WITHOUT EVEN A FIGHT.

THAT'S IT.

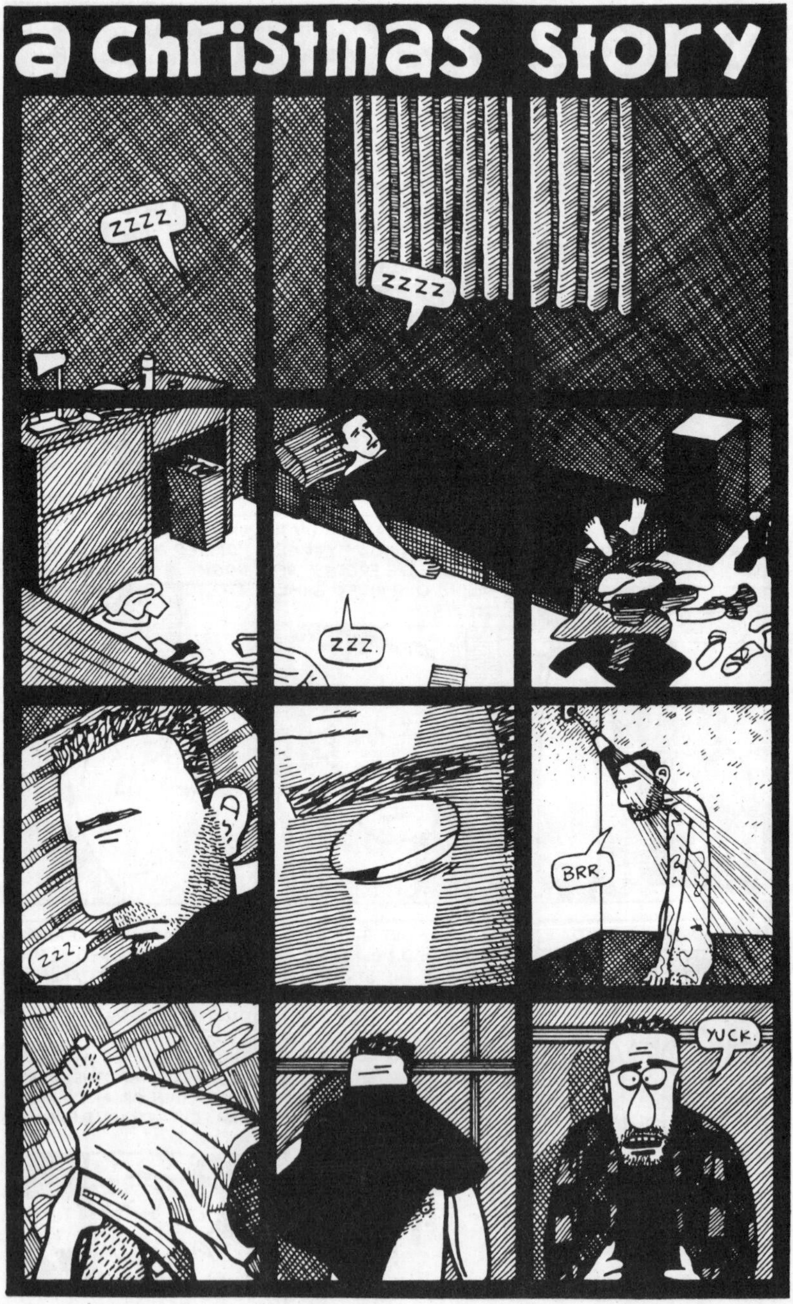
a christmas story
ZZZZ.
ZZZZ
ZZZ.
ZZZ.
BRR.
YUCK.

I WAS DRIVING AROUND WITH MY BROTHER AND TWO FRIENDS.

WE STOPPED AT 7-11 TO BUY SOMETHING OR OTHER.

WHILE WE WERE WAITING IN THE PARKING LOT THREE BLACK MEN PULLED UP, WEARING MASKS AND CARRYING GUNS.

COORS

TWO OF THEM STARTED TO MENACE ALL THE PEOPLE IN THE PARKING LOT (INCLUDING US) WHILE THE OTHER ONE WENT INTO THE STORE.

WHAT SHOULD WE DO?

STAY CALM.

SUDDENLY ONE OF THEM SHOT MY BROTHER IN THE HEAD.

WHAT ARE YOU THINKING?

I'M THINKING STAY CALM... DON'T MOVE.

THE ROBBERS WERE JOKING AROUND... POINTING GUNS AT PEOPLES HEADS... YELLING AT US TO PUT OUR HANDS UP... LAUGHING...

ONE OF THEM POINTED THEIR GUN AT MY HEAD.

PLEASE DON'T...

AS HE PULLED THE TRIGGER I FELT A SEARING PAIN... THEN BLACKNESS.

I DREAMT THIS ON 3.29.94

I WAS ON A LONG UNSUCCESSFUL JOURNEY WITH TWO OF MY BEST FRIENDS.

AFTER MANY ADVENTURES WE FOUND OURSELVES STRANDED ON WHAT WE ASSUMED TO BE A DESERTED ISLAND.

NOW WHAT!

ONE DAY WE FOUND A MAGNIFICENT TREASURE.

HOLY COW!

GULP

WE'RE RICH!

IT CONTAINED GOLD COINS, JEWELS, AND EVEN FRESH GRAPES.

YUM!

WE DUG FOR THREE DAYS AND OUR PILE OF RICHES CONTINUED TO GROW.

WOW!

HOWEVER, LATER THAT DAY WE HEARD A STRANGE NOISE COMING THROUGH THE UNDERGROWTH.

BLOMP, BLOMP

SUDDENLY WE WERE SURROUNDED BY NATIVES WHO PROCEEDED TO TAKE ALL THE TREASURE WE HAD DUG UP (INCLUDING THE DELICIOUS GRAPES).

I NOTICED THAT THE NATIVES APPEARED TO BE LED BY THREE WHITE MEN WHO WERE WATCHING THE SPECTACLE WITH AMUSED EXPRESSIONS.

I GAVE EACH OF THEM ONE OF THE THREE GOLD COINS I WAS HOLDING.

I DREAMT THIS ON 3.28.94

DREAMING
OF A BETTER WORLD

I DECIDED TO TAKE A DAY OFF FROM DRAWING TO DO SOMETHING A LITTLE DIFFERENT.

HI!

MY FRIEND TYLER HAD GOTTEN A BUNCH OF FREE TICKETS TO GO SEE GREEN DAY AT THE CATALYST IN SANTA CRUZ (THANKS TO HIS WACKY CONCERT PRO-MOTER JOB AT COLLEGE).

MAYBE I WASN'T AS EXCIT-ED ABOUT THE SHOW AS I WOULD HAVE BEEN A FEW YEARS AGO, BUT I CAN'T COMPLETELY HATE GREEN DAY JUST BECAUSE THEY SIGNED TO A MAJOR LABEL

I GOT A **FREE** COPY OF THEIR NEW RECORD FROM MY GIRLFRIEND AND I THINK IT'S STILL THE SAME POP/PUNK MUSIC THEY'VE BEEN MAKING FOR YEARS, AND I STILL LIKE IT.

POSER

HOWEVER, I'M **VERY** GLAD I DIDN'T HAVE TO PAY FOR IT AND HELP MAKE WARNER BROTHERS MORE MONEY. I DON'T LIKE MAJOR LABELS, BUT I ESPECIALLY HATE WARNER BECAUSE THEY OWN DC COMICS!

I FIGURED IT WOULD BE INTERESTING TO SEE PEOPLE'S REACTIONS AT A BIG CONCERT PUT ON BY THIS ONCE LITTLE BAND. I WANTED TO SEE WHAT HAPPENS TO A BAND ONCE THEY GET ON MTV.

ALSO I THOUGHT IT WOULD BE A GOOD CHANCE TO SEE SOME OLD FRIENDS THAT I HADN'T SEEN FOR A WHILE...

SO WHEN I WOKE UP I GOT ON A TRAIN BOUND FOR SAN JOSE.

TYLER AND CLAIR MET ME AT THE TRAIN STATION AT TWELVE-THIRTY.

WE WENT OUT TO LUNCH AT THIS WEIRD EXPENSIVE YUPPIE RESTAURANT IN DOWNTOWN SAN JOSE.

IT WAS REALLY GOOD... ESPECIALLY BECAUSE CLAIR PAID.

THANKS!

AFTER LUNCH WE WENT BY SLAVE LABOR GRAPHICS. I SOLD THEM TWENTY COPIES OF MY NEW ZINE AND PICKED UP MY ORIGINAL ARTWORK FROM ISSUE NUMBER THREE OF NO HOPE.

I ALSO GOT A TWENTY-FIVE DOLLAR ROYALTY CHECK FOR MY JANUARY SALES FROM DAN.

IT WAS NICE TO HAVE AT LEAST A LITTLE MONEY IN MY POCKET FOR ONCE.

HAPPY.

WE WENT OVER TO TYLER'S HOUSE AND SPENT A COUPLE OF HOURS LAYING AROUND PLAYING HIS SUPER NINTENDO MACHINE.

AT FIRST IT WAS KIND OF FUN, BUT THEN IT BECAME REALLY BORING.

TYLER HAD TO TAKE CARE OF SOME BUSINESS AT SCHOOL SO I WENT DOWN THERE WITH HIM. AFTER HE WAS DONE WE TRIED TO GO PICK CHRIS UP, BUT HE WASN'T HOME SO WE WENT BACK TO TYLER'S.

BASTARD!

CHRIS WAS ALREADY THERE ALONG WITH PETE, HELEN, AMY, SOME QUIET GUY, CLAIR AND PIZZA.

YUM!

AS WE WERE LEAVING TYLER AND CHRIS STARTED WRESTLING AROUND AND MADE A BIG HOLE IN THE WALL.

CRACK

OH SHIT!   SORRY.

WE MADE IT TO THE SHOW WITHOUT FURTHER INCIDENT.

TILT WAS ALREADY PLAYING. THEY'RE OKAY, BUT AREN'T REALLY DOING ANYTHING NEW OR BETTER THAN ANYBODY ELSE.

THE REST OF THE PEOPLE AT THE CATALYST SEEMED STRANGE TO ME. IT WAS FILLED WITH YOUNG CLEAN CUT LOOKING PEOPLE... FRAT BOY ALTERNATIVE ROCKERS AND HAPPY YOUNG GIRLS. THERE WAS NOBODY THERE WHO LOOKED REMOTELY INTERESTING.

AS SOON AS GREEN DAY TOOK THE STAGE A BIG PIT FORMED.

I WONDERED WHAT IT IS THAT MADE THESE PEOPLE WANT TO RUN IN A CIRCLE AND BASH INTO EACH OTHER. IS IT SOMETHING THEY LEARNED ON MTV? DOES IT MAKE THEM FEEL COOL?

IT SEEMED LIKE THE BAND WAS PRETTY HAPPY TO BE THERE PLAYING TO SO MANY PEOPLE. AFTER YEARS OF HARD WORK IT MUST FEEL NICE TO BE SO SUCCESSFUL.

SOMETIMES THOUGH, IT SEEMED LIKE MOST PEOPLE WEREN'T EVEN PAYING ATTENTION...THAT GREEN DAY WAS JUST THEIR SOUNDTRACK FOR THE NIGHT, SO THEY COULD RUN AROUND AND ACT LIKE MORONS.

HEY- WHY DO PEOPLE AT CONCERTS YELL OUT BAD 70S ROCK SONGS FOR THE BAND TO COVER? THIS SEEMS TO HAPPEN AT EVEN THE PUNKEST SHOWS AT GILMAN ST. IT'S NOT FUNNY!

WHENEVER GREEN DAY PLAYED A CHEEZY COVER, MOST OF THE PEOPLE THERE WENT REALLY CRAZY. ESPECIALLY WHEN THEY PLAYED THE START OF A SLAYER SONG. WHY? TO ME THAT'S EVERYTHING THAT'S BAD ABOUT MUSIC.

FREEBIRD!!!

OVERALL I GUESS I HAD A PRETTY GOOD TIME, BUT THERE WERE JUST TOO MANY BORING PEOPLE THERE, AND THE PLACE WAS JUST TOO BIG FOR ANYTHING UNIQUE TO HAPPEN. MAYBE I'VE JUST BECOME MORE INTERESTED IN OTHER THINGS NOW TO GET TOO EXCITED BY A CONCERT.

WHEN WE LEFT THE SHOW IT HAD STARTED TO RAIN OUTSIDE.

WE ALL DECIDED TO BUY SOME BEER AND MEET BACK AT TYLER'S PLACE.

ON THE WAY HOME TYLER NEARLY CRASHED INTO A GUARDRAIL AND KILLED CHRIS AND ME.

SLOW DOWN! SLOW DOWN!   HUH?

GAH!

WE STAYED UP TALKING FOR AN HOUR OR TWO ABOUT NOTHING IN PARTICULAR AND THEN I FELL ASLEEP.

ZZZ   END.

WHAT THE HELL

I WAS AT MY GRANDMA'S HOUSE IN LOS ANGELES WORKING ON DRAWING COMICS. THERE WAS THIS BIG NOISE LIKE HELICOPTERS FLYING RIGHT OVER THE HOUSE, BUT IT WAS DIFFERENT AND IT JUST KEPT GOING. I WAS TRYING TO IGNORE IT.

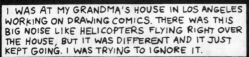

WHAT IS THAT NOISE JEFFREY? I'M REALLY WORRIED! GO OUTSIDE AND SEE WHAT IT IS.

I DON'T HAVE TIME. I HAVE TO FINISH THIS COMIC BY MONDAY. WHY DON'T YOU GO LOOK?

FINE, I WILL!

GOOD!

BREAK A BEER PEACE...

IT'S WEIRD OUT THERE JEFF. I'M NOT SURE WHAT IT IS. THEY LOOK SORT OF LIKE AIRPLANES, BUT THEY HAVE PRO- PELLERS LIKE HELICOPTERS TOO, AND THERE'S A WHOLE BUNCH OF THEM. ...I'M SCARED.

OKAY! OKAY! I'LL GO TAKE A LOOK AND SEE WHAT'S GOING ON. SHIT...

SIGH.

IT WAS PRETTY QUIET ON THE STREET. THERE WERE ONLY THREE LITTLE KIDS PLAYING AROUND ON THEIR BIKES.

IN THE DISTANCE I SAW A WHOLE BUNCH OF WEIRD LIGHTS MOVING AROUND IN THE SKY. IT LOOKED LIKE A WHOLE BUNCH OF PLANES FOLLOWING EACH OTHER, BUT IT WAS DIFFERENT.

SUDDENLY THEY STARTED TO FLY BACK TO WHERE I WAS. I THOUGHT IT WAS GREAT BECAUSE NOW I COULD SEE WHAT THEY WERE, BUT THEY STARTED TO BUZZ SO LOW - RIGHT OVER MY GRANDMA'S HOUSE THAT IT WAS REALLY SCARY.

IT SEEMED LIKE THEY WERE SHOWBOAT-ING AND DOING TRICK FLYING... BUT THEY WEREN'T VERY GOOD.

GULP!

ONE OF THEM CRASHED INTO A TREE RIGHT NEXT TO MY GRANDMA'S HOUSE, THEN ONE OF THEM CRASHED RIGHT INTO IT... CAVING IN PART OF THE FRONT.

I GOT UP EARLY AND PUT THE FINISHING TOUCHES ON A POSTER I HAD TO FINISH FOR THE "ONLY LOCALS ALOUD" CONCERT SERIES AT SJSU THAT MY FRIEND WAS PUTTING ON, THEN I PACKED UP MY BAGS FOR MY TRIP.

AT ELEVEN TYLER ARRIVED AT MY HOUSE. WE SAT AROUND FOR A WHILE UNTIL THE MAIL CAME (YEAH... I'M OBSESSED) THEN WE WENT OUT TO BREAKFAST AT MEL'S.

AFTER BREAKFAST WE DROVE DOWN TO THE EMBARCADERO CENTER AND TRIED OUT ONE OF THOSE NEW VIRTUAL REALITY VIDEO GAMES THAT I HAD JUST READ ABOUT IN THE BAY GUARDIAN.

YOU PUT ON A BULKY HELMET AND THEY WIRE YOU TO A COMPUTER SO ALL YOU SEE IS THE COMPUTER WORLD. IT'S LIKE BEING INSIDE A VIDEO GAME. IN THE ONE WE PLAYED, YOU WALK AROUND A MULTILEVEL CHESS BOARD SHOOTING PEOPLE. I THOUGHT IT WAS PRETTY FUN, BUT MAYBE NOT WORTH FIVE DOLLARS FOR A FOUR MINUTE GAME.

WE STILL HAD A COUPLE OF HOURS TO KILL SO WE DECIDED TO GO TO PIER 39 AND WALK AROUND. IT'S ALWAYS WEIRD TO GO TO THE TOURISTY PARTS OF THIS CITY AND WATCH ALL OF THEM WALKING AROUND CARRYING THEIR CAMERAS AND BEING EXCITED ABOUT EVERY LITTLE THING. I GOT INTO THE SPIRIT AND BOUGHT MYSELF A PRETZEL.

SOON IT WAS TIME TO GET MOVING. TYLER DROVE ME ALL THE WAY TO THE OAKLAND AIRPORT, THEN DROPPED ME OFF.

THANKS TY! I REALLY APPRECIATE THIS. THANKS!

IT'S NO PROBLEM. JUST HAVE A GOOD TRIP!

I WAS PLANNING TO READ ON THE PLANE, BUT ENDED UP JUST FALLING ASLEEP.

ZZZ

AN HOUR AND A HALF LATER, I GOT OFF THE PLANE AND I WAS IN PORTLAND, OREGON. MY MOM, BROTHERS JASON AND MIKE, AND STEP-DAD KEN WERE ALL THERE WAITING FOR ME. I HADN'T SEEN ANY OF THEM (EXCEPT MIKE) IN ALMOST TWO YEARS, BUT THEY ALL LOOKED THE SAME.

OH MY GOD! YOUR HAIR!

RIGHT AWAY (AS WE WERE WALKING TO THE CAR) THEY ALL STARTED ARGUING ABOUT WHERE WE SHOULD GO FOR DINNER. EVENTUALLY WE ENDED UP AT THIS PRETTY COOL ITALIAN PLACE IN EAST PORTLAND.

DINNER WAS GOOD. IT WAS FUN TO BE TO-GETHER ALMOST LIKE A REAL FAMILY, THE JOKING AROUND AND BANTER CAME EASY. THE SALAD I HAD WASN'T BAD EITHER.

AFTER DINNER, WE ALL DROVE TO MY MOM'S HOUSE IN TIGARD (WHERE I WAS GOING TO STAY). WE HAD A BIG TREAT OF GRASS-HOPPER PIE FOR DESSERT.

FOR A FEW MORE HOURS WE STAYED UP TALKING, THEN JASON WENT HOME AND EVERYONE ELSE WENT TO SLEEP. I STAYED UP WATCHING A CHARLIE CHAPLIN VIDEO THAT THEY HAD, FOR A WHILE , THEN WENT TO SLEEP MYSELF.

I SLEPT IN LATE THE NEXT MORNING AND BY THE TIME I WOKE UP, NOBODY WAS AROUND. MY MOM WAS AT WORK, MIKE WAS AT SCHOOL AND KEN WAS IN HIS WORK SHED IN THE BACKYARD (WHERE HE MAKES REALLY EXPENSIVE, COLLECTABLE GLASS PAPERWEIGHTS).

AFTER I TOOK A SHOWER I GOT A PHONE-CALL FROM MY "REAL" DAD. HE SAID HE KNEW I DIDN'T REALLY WANT TO SEE HIM AND DIDN'T HAVE MUCH FREE TIME, BUT THAT HE HAD SOMETHING IMPORTANT THAT HE WANTED TO TALK TO ME ABOUT.

OKAY...OKAY...WE'LL HAVE A QUICK LUNCH, BUT I GOTTA BE BACK HERE BY 12:30 'CAUSE I HAVE A DENTIST APPOINTMENT AT ONE AND MY MOM IS TAKING ME.

SO MY DAD (WHO I HADN'T TALKED TO IN ABOUT A YEAR) CAME (ALONG WITH MY BROTHER JASON, WHO LIVES WITH HIM STILL) AND TOOK ME OUT TO LUNCH.

HI!

HI.

THE TRUTH IS, I NEVER LIKED MY DAD MUCH, BUT BY THE END OF THIS LUNCH I ENDED UP HATING HIS GUTS MORE THAN ANY OTHER PERSON I'VE EVER KNOWN.

AS SOON AS WE SAT DOWN AT OUR TABLE HE SAID –

THIS ISN'T A LECTURE... MAYBE YOU'LL THINK IT'S ONE, BUT IT'S NOT. FOR A LONG TIME I'VE BEEN WANTING TO EXPLAIN TO YOU MY SIDE OF THINGS ABOUT YOUR MOTHER'S AND MY DIVORCE AND ABOUT MY RELATIONSHIP TO YOU OVER THE YEARS, AND THE WAY THINGS HAVE TURNED OUT. I THINK NOW YOU ARE PROBABLY OLD ENOUGH TO UNDERSTAND EVERYTHING I HAVE TO SAY...

AND HE PROCEEDED TO LECTURE ME FOR THE NEXT HOUR AND A HALF.

IN THOSE DAYS THERE WAS A LOT OF THAT FOOLISH WOMEN'S LIBERATION TALK... AND YOUR MOTHER'S PSYCHOLOGIST WAS ENCOURAGING HER TO GET A DIVORCE SO SHE COULD BE HER OWN PERSON.

NOW, I ALWAYS BELIEVED THAT THE MARRIAGE VOWS WERE A SACRED THING, AND I MEANT IT WHEN I SAID TILL DEATH DO US PART... BUT THAT'S NOT HOW YOUR MOTHER FELT. PLUS, HER BOSS AT WORK WANTED TO HAVE A MORE THAN PROFESSIONAL RELATIONSHIP WITH HER, IF YOU KNOW WHAT I MEAN...

WINK

WINK

ONCE SHE MOVED OUT AND WE WERE DIVORCED, I DECIDED TO START RAISING YOU KIDS THE RIGHT WAY... YOU BOTH HAD A LOT OF BAD HABITS AND WERE SPOILED... YOUR DIETS WERE HORRIBLE. I REMEMBER ONE PARTICULARLY FUNNY INSTANCE WHEN YOUR BROTHER REFUSED TO EAT HIS APPLESAUCE AND I MADE HIM KEEP IT IN HIS MOUTH FOR OVER TWO HOURS UNTIL HE FINALLY SWALLOWED IT.

HA HA!

YOU AND YOUR MOTHER HAD A VERY STRANGE ATTRACTION TO EACH OTHER... I WOULD ALMOST SAY IT WAS PERVERSE. SHE WAS USING YOU TO SUBVERT OUR NEW FAMILY... IMPLANTING IDEAS INTO YOUR HEAD.

YOU WERE A VERY DISTURBED CHILD... WHICH IS WHY WE SENT YOU TO A PSYCHIATRIST... TO TRY TO UNDO YOUR MOTHER'S BRAIN-WASHING. BUT IT WASN'T WORKING... WHICH IS WHY I DECIDED YOU COULD MOVE IN WITH HER. I KNEW ONE OF TWO THINGS WOULD HAPPEN... EITHER YOU WOULD REALIZE HOW MESSED UP SHE WAS, OR YOU WOULD TURN INTO ANOTHER HER AND NEVER GROW UP INTO A GOOD PERSON.

ON AND ON HE WENT... WITH HIS TALE GETTING MORE AND MORE BIZARRE BY THE SECOND. I NEVER REALIZED QUITE COMPLETELY HOW FUCKED UP HE WAS UNTIL THAT MEAL. I WANTED TO STAB HIM IN THE FACE, BUT INSTEAD I TRIED TO EAT AND SAID NOTHING.

WHEN HE FINALLY DROPPED JASON AND ME BACK AT MY MOM'S HOUSE (LATE) I SAID...

I DON'T REGRET ANY DECISION I EVER MADE... ESPECIALLY THE ONE TO LEAVE YOU AND TO GO LIVE WITH MY MOM.

THEN HE LEFT... AND I SWEAR, I HOPE I NEVER SEE HIM AGAIN.

WE MADE IT TO THE DENTIST'S OFFICE JUST IN TIME. UNFORTUNATELY, ONCE THEY FINISHED CLEANING MY TEETH, I WAS INFORMED I HAD TWO CAVITIES.

THE DOCTOR HAD TWO CANCELLATIONS, SO I WAS ABLE TO GET THEM FILLED RIGHT THEN. FOR A BIRTHDAY GIFT, MY MOM PAID. IT WASN'T MUCH FUN. FOR ONE OF THE FILLINGS THEY DIDN'T USE ANY NOVOCAINE OR ANYTHING.

AFTER THAT WONDERFUL EXPERIENCE, MY MOM WENT BACK TO WORK AND MY BROTHER AND I WENT TO DOWNTOWN PORTLAND AND SPENT THE REST OF THE AFTERNOON LOOKING THROUGH SOME PRETTY COOL BOOKSTORES.

WE GOT BACK TO MY MOM'S HOUSE AT SEVEN AND HAD DINNER. ONCE AGAIN WE ALL STAYED UP TALKING UNTIL LATE IN THE NIGHT.

ON FRIDAY MORNING, I WOKE UP TO A DESERTED HOUSE. I WATCHED A COUPLE MORE CHAPLIN SHORTS, READ A LITTLE, AND EVEN TRIED TO DO A LITTLE DRAWING, BUT COULDN'T GET INTO IT. FOR SOME REASON, IT'S REALLY HARD FOR ME TO CONCENTRATE ON DRAWING COMICS UNLESS I'M IN MY OWN ROOM, WORKING AT MY OWN DESK.

AT AROUND ONE, MY MOM CAME HOME AND WE WENT OUT FOR A GREAT LUNCH. BACK WHEN I WAS A TEENAGER, I HAD SO MANY PROBLEMS WITH MY MOM, BUT IN THE LAST COUPLE OF YEARS WE'VE BEEN GETTING ALONG A LOT BETTER AND IT'S BECOME REALLY FUN TO HANG OUT WITH HER, NOW THAT WE'RE ON MORE EQUAL GROUND (I.E. SHE CAN'T TELL ME WHAT TO DO ANYMORE).

AFTER LUNCH WE WENT TO PICK UP MIKE FROM SCHOOL, THEN WE ALL WENT TO THEIR GIANT SUPERMARKET (FRED MYERS). NOT SURPRISINGLY, SHOPPING WITH THEM FOR GROCERIES ENDED UP BEING PRETTY BORING.

AT AROUND EIGHT O'CLOCK, MY MOM DROPPED ME DOWNTOWN SO I COULD MEET UP WITH MY GIRLFRIEND LISA. SHE'D BEEN ON TOUR WITH HER BAND, IDA, AND THEY WERE HAVING A SHOW THAT NIGHT AT THE X-RAY CAFE.

HEY MAN, WANT SOME H? I CAN FIX YOU UP...I'LL EVEN GIVE YOU A FREE TASTE... IT'S GOOD SHIT.

NO THANKS.

I WAITED AROUND FOR ABOUT HALF AN HOUR. AT LAST THEY ARRIVED. IT WAS REALLY GREAT TO SEE LISA ONCE AGAIN.

THEY LOADED IN, THEN LISA AND I WENT IN SEARCH OF FOOD. EVERYTHING SEEMED TO BE CLOSED, BUT FINALLY WE FOUND A CHINESE PLACE AND I BOUGHT US SOME RICE, BROCCOLI AND TOFU TO GO.

I THOUGHT THE SHOW WENT PRETTY GOOD, EVEN IF A LOT OF PEOPLE WEREN'T THERE BECAUSE THE HEADLINING BAND (THE EXCELLENT UNWOUND) HAD CANCELLED TO PLAY A BETTER PAYING SHOW AT REED COLLEGE.

AFTER THE SHOW, THE REST OF THE BAND WENT TO SOME GUY'S HOUSE AND LISA AND I TOOK A CAB ALL THE WAY BACK TO MY MOM'S PLACE.

WE SPENT THE NEXT MORNING RELAXING AROUND THE HOUSE. LISA DID HER LAUNDRY AND TRIED TO FIND OUT IF THEY WERE GOING TO BE INTERVIEWED ON A LOCAL RADIO STATION OR NOT.

AFTER MUCH WAITING AROUND, THE INTERVIEW ENDED UP NOT HAPPENING, SO WE WENT OUT FOR A LATE LUNCH WITH MY MOM AND KEN. SINCE MY MOM HAD NEVER MET LISA BEFORE, SHE GOT THE CHANCE TO HUMILIATE ME BY RELATING EMBARRASSING MOMENTS FROM MY CHILDHOOD.

...AND ALL THE TIME THERE USED TO BE ROACHES IN THE SHOWER IN THE MORNING, BUT JEFF WAS AFRAID OF THEM... SO HE'D WAKE ME UP SO I WOULD KILL THEM FOR HIM. HEE HEE HEE! SNORT!

HA HA!!!

GROAN...

ACTUALLY THOUGH, LUNCH WAS A LOT OF FUN. AFTERWARDS, THEY DROPPED US IN DOWNTOWN PORTLAND. WE WENT TO A COMIC BOOK STORE WHERE LISA SOLD SEVEN COPIES OF HER COMIC, BUT WE SPENT MOST OF THE AFTERNOON LOOKING AROUND POWELLS... A HUGE (ONE CITY BLOCK BIG) BOOKSTORE. IT EVEN HAS ITS OWN COFFEE SHOP, WHERE WE SHARED A PEANUT BUTTER COOKIE.

AT AROUND EIGHT, WE MET UP WITH THE REST OF THE BAND AND HELPED LOAD THEIR EQUIPMENT INTO THE CLUB THEY WERE PLAYING AT. IT WAS THE NU BONE, AND IT WAS A PRETTY LAME PLACE... BIG... AND BLACK... AND OH SO VERY ALTERNATIVE.

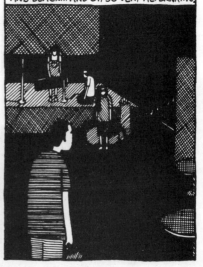

ONCE AGAIN, THE ORIGINALLY HEADLINING BAND CANCELLED SO HARDLY ANYBODY WAS THERE, BUT MY MOM CAME... AND EVEN MY BROTHER JASON. I THOUGHT THAT WAS PRETTY COOL.

AFTER IDA PLAYED, I SAID GOODBYE TO LISA (THEY WERE HEADING BACK TO SAN FRANCISCO AFTER THE SHOW BECAUSE THEY HAD TO GET THE VAN THEY'D RENTED BACK AT A CERAIN TIME) AND I WENT HOME WITH MY MOM AND JASON.

IT WAS GOOD TO SEE YOU. I LOVE YOU.

I LOVE YOU TOO.

THE NEXT MORNING WAS A SPECIAL MORNING... BECAUSE IT WAS THE LAST DAY OF MY VISIT BEFORE I HAD TO HEAD HOME AND GET BACK TO REAL LIFE. MY MOM MADE ME THE SPECIAL TREAT FROM MY YOUTH OF MATZO PANCAKES - ONE OF THE VERY BEST THINGS IN THE WORLD!

FOR MOST OF THE DAY WE JUST TOOK IT EASY AROUND THE HOUSE...

I FEEL LIKE SUCH A SLOTH... WE'RE JUST LAYING HERE DOING NOTHING. DON'T YOU WANT TO DO SOMETHING?

NAH. IT'S NICE TO RELAX. ANY-WAY, WHAT IS THERE TO DO?

ACTUALLY, WE DID GO OUT FOR A LITTLE BIT...TO FRED MYERS...WHERE MY MOM BOUGHT ME A NEW ELECTRIC RAZOR. THEN WE WENT BACK TO POWELL'S BOOKS, WHERE I BOUGHT TWO SPECIAL BOOKS I KNEW LISA WANTED FOR HER BIRTHDAY (WHICH WAS THREE DAYS AWAY).

DON'T YOU WANT TO GET HER SOMETHING NICE... LIKE PERFUME...OR A CARD?

ER...I DON'T KNOW MOM...

...AND THEN TO THE AIRPORT, WHICH WAS REALLY CROWDED. WHILE I WAS GETTING READY TO BOARD THE PLANE, MY MOM STARTED TO CRY, AND I FELT REALLY SAD TOO. I'D HAD A GREAT TIME (EXCEPT FOR LUNCH WITH MY DAD) AND WISHED I COULDA STAYED LONGER. IT WAS GREAT SEEING MY MOM AND MIKE TOGETHER AGAIN, AND MISS THE OLD DAYS WHEN WE ALL LIVED IN THE SAME HOUSE... ESPECIALLY CAUSE I KNOW THOSE DAYS ARE GONE FOREVER.

I BARELY MANAGED TO KEEP MYSELF FROM CRYING TOO AS I GOT ON THE PLANE AND WAVED GOODBYE.

AN HOUR AND A HALF LATER, I LANDED BACK IN OAKLAND. I TOOK THE BUS TO BART AND THEN BART BACK TO SAN FRANCISCO. THEN I HOPPED ON THE N JUDAH TO CARL AND COLE AND WALKED THE REST OF THE WAY TO LISA'S HOUSE. NOT MUCH LATER WE WENT TO SLEEP.

THE END.

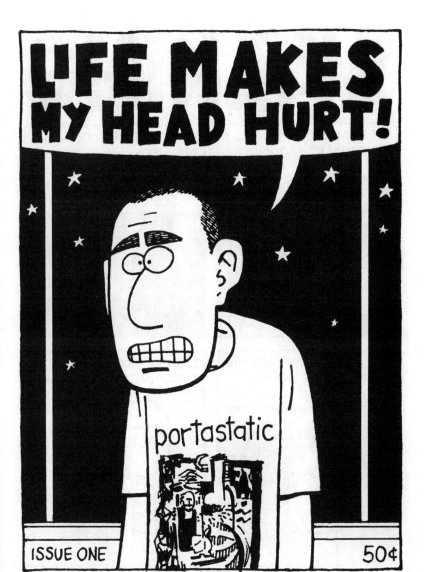

WALKING

I'M ALWAYS TAKING REALLY LONG WALKS AROUND THE CITY.

SOMETIMES I START WALKING WHEN I WAKE UP AND DON'T COME BACK HOME UNTIL I NEED TO GO BACK TO SLEEP.

WHILE I WALK I TRY TO THINK ABOUT WHAT'S WRONG WITH MY LIFE AND WHAT I HAVE TO DO TO MAKE IT BETTER.

I NEVER SUCCEED IN FINDING ANY SOLUTIONS.

END.

A DREAM

I DREAMT I WAS A BIRD.

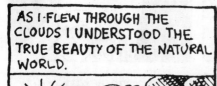

AS I FLEW THROUGH THE CLOUDS I UNDERSTOOD THE TRUE BEAUTY OF THE NATURAL WORLD.

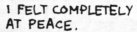

I FELT COMPLETELY AT PEACE.

ACTUALLY I'M LYING. I HAD NO SUCH DREAM.

END.

HOW I BECAME UNEMPLOYED #7

A FEW YEARS AGO I HAD A JOB IN A SURPLUS ELECTRONIC PARTS WAREHOUSE.

I SPENT EIGHT HOURS A DAY PULLING ORDERS... PUTTING THE RIGHT NUMBER OF PARTS INTO LITTLE BAGS.

THE ORDER PACKERS HAD A RADIO THAT YOU HEARD THROUGH OUT THE WHOLE WAREHOUSE... AND UNFORTUNATELY THEY HAD REALLY BAD TASTE.

I DIDN'T THINK THAT IT WAS FAIR THAT EVERYBODY HAD TO LISTEN TO THEIR CRAPPY MUSIC. EVERYDAY I WENT HOME WITH A HEADACHE.

SUNDAYS

SUNDAY HAS ALWAYS BEEN MY FAVORITE DAY.

THE DAY OF REST!

WHEN I WAS GROWING UP I'D SPEND SUNDAYS OVER AT MY MOM'S HOUSE. MY BROTHER AND I WOULD GET UP EARLY AND WATCH CARTOONS ON CHANNEL 5.

IN THOSE DAYS THEY PLAYED 5 HOURS OF OLD POPEYE CARTOONS EVERY SUNDAY ON A GREAT SHOW HOSTED BY TOM PATTON... AND MIXED BETWEEN THE POPEYE SHORTS THEY SHOWED EPISODES OF SUPERCHICKEN, GEORGE OF THE JUNGLE AND TOM SLICK.

I YAM WHAT I YAM!

SOME OF THE BEST SUNDAYS OF MY LIFE WERE DURING THE YEAR I LIVED WITH MY FRIENDS CHRIS AND ROBIN SAN JOSE.

EVERYBODY SLEPT IN LATE AND THEN WE'D SPEND A COUPLE OF HOURS CLEANING THE APARTMENT AND BLASTING OLD REPLACEMENTS OR DINOSAUR JR. RECORDS.

WHEN WE WERE DONE WE'D GO BUY A TWELVE PACK OR TWO.

FOR THE REST OF THE DAY WE WOULD JUST SIT AROUND, RELAX, AND LISTEN TO GREAT MUSIC.

THUMB!

AS MUCH AS I MISS THOSE DAYS... I HAVE TO ADMIT... THINGS ARE EVEN BETTER RIGHT NOW.

SUNDAY IS THE ONE DAY OF EACH WEEK THAT BOTH MY GIRLFRIEND LISA AND I DON'T HAVE TO WORK AND WE USUALLY HANG OUT TOGETHER ALL DAY.

SOMETIMES WE GO SEE A MOVIE OR GO FOR A WALK, AND WE USUALLY GO GET A GOOD MEAL AT THE PARADISO CAFE.

...AND SOMETIMES WE'LL JUST LAY IN BED ALL DAY.

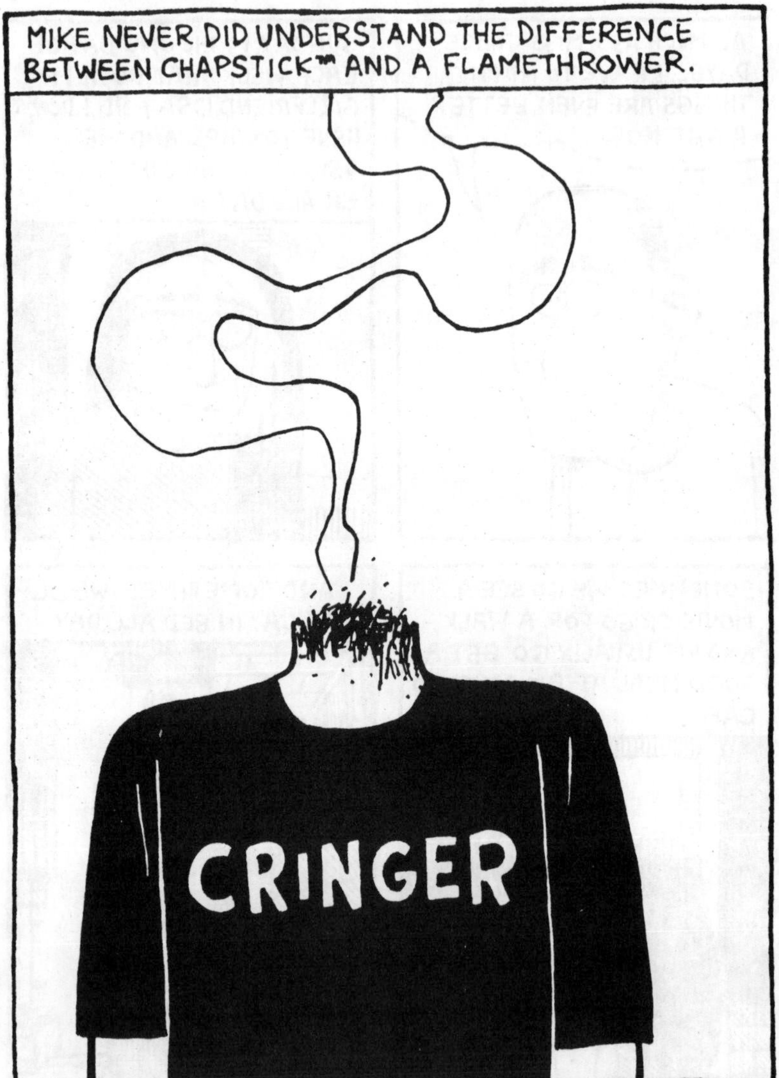
MIKE NEVER DID UNDERSTAND THE DIFFERENCE BETWEEN CHAPSTICK™ AND A FLAMETHROWER.
CRINGER

THE DRESSER

I DECIDED TO WALK THE TWO BLOCKS TO MY HOUSE, AND GIVE MYSELF A LITTLE TIME TO THINK ABOUT IT.

SURE, SEVENTY BUCKS IS A LOT OF MONEY, BUT IT WAS EXACTLY WHAT I NEEDED. NOT ONLY WOULD I HAVE A PLACE TO STORE MY CLOTHES, BUT NOW I'D ALSO HAVE A PLACE TO KEEP MY BOOKS.

I PACED AND PACED, BUT COULDN'T COME TO A DECISION.

AFTER ABOUT HALF AN HOUR, MY FRIEND CHRIS SHOWED UP AND WE DROVE TO BERKELEY TO SEE SOME STUPID PUNK SHOW AT GILMAN ST.

I NEVER DID GET THAT DRESSER, AND MY ROOM IS STILL A MESS. I GUESS I REALLY SHOULD HAVE TRIED HAGGLING ON THE PRICE.

FOR THE LOSERS

AT FIRST IT LOOKED LIKE IT WAS GOING TO BE JUST ANOTHER REGULAR DAY AT SIXTY-THREE SOUTH NINTH STREET. LITTLE DID ANYBODY BEGIN TO REALIZE THE INCREDIBLE EVENTS THAT WERE IN STORE FOR OUR PATHETIC HEROES.

DARKNESS

EVERY DAY I WAKE UP AT EXACTLY SIX IN THE MORNING.

THE FIRST THING I ALWAYS DO IS TAKE A HOT SHOWER. IT HELPS TO WAKE ME UP.

NEXT I MASTURBATE. I DON'T WANT TO BE WALKING AROUND WORK ALL DAY WITH A BIG HARD-ON... PLUS IT FEELS GOOD.

THEN I EAT A BOWL OF FROSTED FLAKES CEREAL IN COLD MILK. THEY'RE MY FAVORITE! I KNOW THAT THEY'RE NOT JUST FOR KIDS.

AT SEVEN O'CLOCK I GET IN MY CAR AND BEGIN MY COMMUTE.

I WORK IN PALO ALTO SO TRAFFIC IS ALWAYS REALLY BAD. I DON'T MIND TOO MUCH THOUGH. I JUST ROLL UP MY WINDOWS AND LISTEN TO CLASSIC ROCK RADIO ON MY CAR STEREO.

WORK STARTS AT EIGHT-THIRTY. I DE-BUG COMPUTER PROGRAMS.

IT CAN BE KIND OF BORING, BUT AT LEAST I HAVE MY OWN CUBICLE.

I'VE BEEN WORKING HERE FOR SEVEN YEARS. IT'S A GOOD COMPANY. LAST YEAR THEY GAVE ME A TWO HUNDRED DOLLAR CHRISTMAS BONUS.

MOSTLY I JUST SIT IN MY CUBICLE AND DO MY JOB. I DON'T SOCIALIZE MUCH WITH THE OTHER EMPLOYEES.

ONCE I ASKED MY CO-WORKER JANET OUT ON A DATE TO GO SEE THE DISNEY MOVIE ALADDIN, BUT SHE SAID NO.

SHE'S SO BEAUTIFUL. I HAVE FANTASIES ABOUT HER ALL THE TIME. I'M TRYING TO GET UP THE COURAGE TO ASK HER OUT AGAIN.

AT FIVE O'CLOCK I PUNCH OUT AND GET BACK IN MY CAR FOR THE DRIVE HOME.

ONCE I GET HOME, I MAKE MYSELF A TURKEY POT PIE FOR DINNER AND WATCH TV. BLOSSOM IS MY FAVORITE SHOW, BUT I'M NOT SURE WHY.

I USUALLY GO TO SLEEP AT ELEVEN. I WISH I HAD ENOUGH ENERGY TO STAY UP TO WATCH THE JAY LENO SHOW, BUT I JUST GET TOO TIRED.

PRETTY MUCH EVERY DAY IS EXACTLY LIKE THIS.

THE END.

WEIRD HAIR

NIGHTMARE

LAST NIGHT I DREAMED I HAD LONG DREADLOCKED HAIR.

IT WAS ONE OF THE VERY WORST DREAMS I'VE EVER HAD.

END.

WHITE NIGHT

I HAD A DREAM THAT I WAS WALKING DOWN THE STREET WITH A BUNCH OF FRIENDS.

UP AHEAD A NAZI STARTED YELLING AT ME.

FUCK YOU...GODDAMN JEWBOY! YOU'RE GONNA DIE, YOU BIG NOSED, MONEY GRUBBING SMELLY, BACKWARDS MOTHERFUCKER!

AT FIRST WE TRIED TO IGNORE HIM, BUT THEN I REALIZED...

I DON'T HAVE TO TAKE THIS CRAP!

I RAN UP TO THE NAZI SCUMBAG, AND BEGAN BEATING HIM SENSELESS.

POW

HEY!

HEY, OW! STOP! OW!!! STOP, YOU FUCKING JEW! I WAS ONLY JOKING! AREN'T YOU PEOPLE SUPPOSED TO BE FUNNY? OW!

MY FRIENDS JUST KEPT WALKING, AND I KEPT POUNDING ON THE FUCKER.

CRUNCH

OUT OF NOWHERE THIS HUGE NAZI APPEARED AND STOMPED ME.

GAH!

END

...AND THE DAYS GO BY LIKE BROKEN RECORDS

JUNE 17th, 1994... TAKE A GOOD LOOK, BECAUSE THIS PLACE MAY WELL BE HELL.

KAISER

FOR THE LAST FOUR DAYS LISA'S SIDE, NEAR HER APPENDIX, HAS BEEN REAL HURTING AND TODAY I FINALLY MANAGED TO CONVINCE HER TO GO TO KAISER (WHERE SHE'S A MEMBER) BLAINE GAVE US A RIDE THERE, AND THEN THE WAITING BEGAN.

SHE WAS PROBED, POKED AND EXAMINED IN EVERY WAY IMAGINABLE... AND I WAIT AND WORRIED.

AFTER MANY HOURS SHE FINALLY RE-EMERGED...

WELL, WHAT DID THEY SAY? WHAT IS IT?

THEY SAID THEY DON'T KNOW WHAT IT IS. IF IT GETS ANY WORSE WE'RE SUPPOSED TO COME BACK.

AIEE! YES, THIS IS HELL.

JUNE 28th, 1994... I WOKE UP AT SEVEN O'CLOCK TO GO DOWN TO SAN JOSE AND HELP MAKE THE NEW SLAVE LABOR CATALOG... I NEED MONEY.

I WAS HOPING TO GET SOME SLEEP ON THE TRAIN, SINCE I'D ONLY HAD FIVE HOURS SLEEP, BUT I COULDN'T FALL ASLEEP AND READ INSTEAD.

THE CATALOG IS ENDING UP COMING OUT PRETTY NICE. FOR A FREE COPY YOU CAN CALL SLAVE LABOR TOLL FREE AT 1-800-866-8929.

CHRIS PICKED ME UP FROM WORK, THEN WE MET SOOZ AND WENT OUT TO DINNER. CHRIS AND SOOZ ARE GOOD PEOPLE.

AFTER DINNER CHRIS AND I PLAYED BASKET-BALL AND LISTENED TO MUSIC IN HIS BACK-YARD FOR HOURS AND HOURS. EVERY NIGHT SHOULD BE LIKE THIS.

JULY 2nd, 1994... A COUPLE OF WEEKS AGO I GOT A NEW JOB AND I ACTUALLY LIKE IT.

AFTER YEARS OF WORKING SHITTY TELEMARKETING JOBS, WORKING IN FUCKED UP WAREHOUSES, AND WORSE, WHO WOULD HAVE THOUGHT I WOULD HAVE FOUND TRUE HAPPINESS WORKING IN A COMIC BOOK STORE?

YEAH, THERE'S A LOT OF ANNOYING SHIT, LIKE ALL THE PEOPLE WHO COME HERE TO BUY LEGEND CARDS FOR THAT STUPID MAGIC GAME, BUT THIS IS DEFINITELY THE BEST JOB I'VE EVER HAD.

JULY 24th 1994...
TODAY WAS THE
FIRST WARM DAY
IN A MONTH. IT'S
BEEN SO COLD AND
CLOUDY ALL SUMMER,
IT WAS REALLY NICE
TO FINALLY SEE THE
SUN.

UNFORTUNATELY I SPENT
THE WHOLE DAY AT WORK.
I GOT OFF AT 7:40, JUST
IN TIME FOR SUNSET.

I BOUGHT A PIECE OF PIZZA AND
WALKED HOME EATING IT.

BLAH... THIS TASTES
LIKE CARDBOARD.

LISA AND I GOT INTO A STUPID ARGU-
MENT ON THE PHONE. I GOT IN SUCH A
BAD MOOD THAT INSTEAD OF WORKING
ON COMICS I JUST WATCHED THE
DODGERS BEAT THE GIANTS TEN TO
FIVE ON TV.

ANYWAY, IT'S HARD TO GET UP THE ENERGY
TO WORK ON ANY COMICS AFTER WORKING
ALL DAY IN A COMIC BOOK STORE.

JULY 25th, 1994... UHG! NOT ANOTHER PUNK ROCK SHOW. LISA DRAGGED ME TO THIS ONE PRACTICALLY AGAINST MY WILL.

LATELY, THERE'S NOTHING LESS FUN THAN BEING SURROUNDED BY DRUNK, SMOKING POSERS BEING "PUNK ROCK," AND LISTENING TO MUSIC FAR TOO LOUD FOR THE HUMAN EAR. I'M JUST PLAIN SICK OF SEEING SHOWS, AND HOPEFULLY I'LL NEVER HAVE TO GO TO ANOTHER ONE AGAIN. I'D MUCH RATHER JUST LISTEN TO A CD IN THE COMFORT OF MY OWN HOUSE.

ACTUALLY, I HAVE TO ADMIT, I ENDED UP ENJOYING JAWBOX, BUT THIS TIME AROUND JAWBREAKER JUST PLAIN STUNK (WHICH WAS WEIRD, AS NORMALLY THEY'RE ONE OF MY VERY FAVORITE BANDS). WELL, ATLEAST WE GOT IN FOR FREE.

JULY 29th, 1994... ONE OF MY LEAST FAVORITE THINGS TO DO IS LAUNDRY.

UNFORTUNATELY IT'S UNAVOIDABLE... EVERY WEEK AND A HALF OR SO I HAVE TO TREK DOWN TO THE LAUNDROMAT, MY DUFFEL BAG IN TOW.

I DON'T LIKE MY LAUNDROMAT AT ALL. IT'S TOO EXPENSIVE AND ALL THE MACHINES ARE OLD AND FALLING APART.

TODAY I PUT ONE DOLLAR INTO THE WASHER AND ABSOLUTELY NOTHING HAPPENED, SO I HAD TO LOAD EVERYTHING INTO ANOTHER MACHINE AND WASTE AN EXTRA DOLLAR.

THE WORST PART ABOUT DOING LAUNDRY IS THE WAITING. YOU CAN'T LEAVE BECAUSE MAYBE SOMEBODY WILL STEAL ALL YOUR CLOTHES, BUT THERE'S NOTHING TO DO WHILE YOU WAIT. SUCCESS TO ME, WILL BE HAVING MY OWN WASHER AND DRYER IN MY HOUSE.

AUGUST 6th 1994. TODAY IN SAN DIEGO I SAW ONE OF THE MOST BIZARRE THINGS I'VE EVER SEEN IN MY LIFE.

THIS WOMAN HONESTLY BELIEVES SHE IS ACTUALLY UNDERDOG.

SEPTEMBER 6th, 1994...

END.

THE ROCK

ONCE THERE WAS A ROCK WHO LIVED ON THE GROUND.

IT WAS A VERY LONELY ROCK, AND VERY DISSATISFIED WITH IT'S EXISTENCE.

ONE DAY THE ROCK DECIDED TO KILL ITSELF.

THE ROCK THOUGHT AND THOUGHT, BUT WAS UNABLE TO FIGURE OUT A WAY TO END ITS LIFE.

... SO IT'S PATHETIC LIFE CONTINUED FOREVER, AND IT WAS NEVER HAPPY.

end

SATURDAY

I WAKE UP COLD AND ALONE.

DAMN IT...YET AGAIN, I'VE SLEPT TOO LATE TO WATCH ANY CARTOONS.

THERE'S BARELY ENOUGH TIME TO TAKE A SHOWER AND RUSH TO WORK.

THIS GODDAMN JOB IS KILLING ME! IT'S SUCKING AWAY MY LIFE... AND FOR ONLY FIVE BUCKS AN HOUR!

I CAN'T SMILE... I CAN'T SMILE...

I HATE THE CUSTOMERS.

WHERE DO YOU KEEP YOUR VERTIGO COMIC BOOKS?

I HATE MY BOSS.

LATE AGAIN, EH LEVINE?

I HATE EVERYBODY!

JUST WHEN IT SEEMS LIKE THE WORK DAY IS NEVER GOING TO END, IT FINALLY DOES.

SORRY WE'RE CLOSED

MY TEETH, HEAD AND BACK HURT. I'M EXHAUSTED.

I WALK HOME AVOIDING THE HIPPIES AND HOME-LESS FUCKS AS BEST AS I CAN.

SPARA A JUANA?

I FALL ASLEEP COLD AND ALONE.

END.

AGAIN WITH THE COMICS

SOMETIMES I THINK I'M THE MOST PATHETIC PERSON TO WALK THE FACE OF THE EARTH.

I MEAN, MY WHOLE LIFE IS COMICS!

NOT ONLY DO I MAKE MY OWN MAGAZINE ABOUT COMICS...

DESTROY ALL COMICS

ISSUE ONE $3.50

NOT ONLY DO I DRAW COMICS...

BUT I ALSO WORK IN A COMIC BOOK STORE.

FOR ENTERTAINMENT, IN MY FREE TIME, I READ COMICS.

SOMETIMES I EVEN DREAM ABOUT COMICS!

HELP! WILL SOMEBODY OUT THERE PLEASE SHOOT ME?

END. J.L. 10.94

LOST IN A LAND WITHOUT HOPE

©1994 JEFF LEVINE

AFTER I GOT OUT OF MY SHITTY TELEMARKETING JOB SELLING NEWSPAPERS, AND RODE THE BUS HOME...

I GOT A BEER OUT OF THE FRIDGE,

PUT JAWBREAKER ON THE TURNTABLE,

SAT DOWN ON THE COUCH,

...AND IT ALMOST MADE LIFE SEEM WORTHWHILE.

END

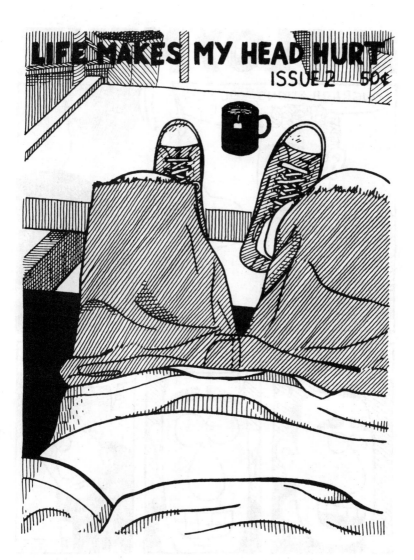

EMPLOYMENT

REOCCURRING FANTASY

I'M IN A RESTAURANT, EATING A BURRITO.

SUDDENLY SOMEBODY GRABS MY BACKPACK AND RUNS OUT.

STOP!

I CHASE AFTER HIM THROUGH THE STREETS

REACHING INTO MY POCKET I PULL OUT MY KNIFE.

EVENTUALLY I CATCH HIM, AND STAB HIM TO DEATH.

END.

THE MISSING PIECES

6.4.94... **WHY HAVE I BEEN SO DEPRESSED TODAY?** TO MOST PEOPLE IT MUST LOOK AS THOUGH I'VE GOT A PRETTY GOOD LIFE. I MEAN, I'VE GOT A ROOF OVER MY HEAD, AND FOOD IN MY STOMACH. FOR THE FIRST TIME IN MY LIFE I'M IN LOVE WITH A GIRL WHO LOVES ME TOO. I EVEN GOT THREE LETTERS IN THE MAIL TODAY! **I JUST WISH I COULD FIGURE OUT WHY I FEEL LIKE TOTAL SHIT!!!** NO MATTER WHAT I ACCOMPLISH I'M NEVER SATISFIED! ONE OF THE LETTERS I GOT TODAY SAID I SHOULD BE HAPPY THAT ATLEAST I CAN DRAW. THE PROBLEM IS, THAT DOESN'T MAKE ME HAPPY, BECAUSE I DON'T THINK I **CAN** DRAW. COMPARED TO ANYBODY ELSE'S COMICS I LOOK AT, I THINK MINE LOOK LIKE COMPLETE CRAP (WELL, ALMOST ANYBODY'S). AT THE BEST I'M MEDIOCRE. I NEED TO GET A REAL JOB. I NEED TO SHAVE.

7.3.94

I SPENT THE DAY OVER AT LISA'S HOUSE, TRYING TO COME UP WITH SOME IDEAS FOR COMICS. SHE'S BEEN LETTING ME STAY HERE BECAUSE I ALREADY MOVED OUT OF MY OLD HOUSE, BUT CAN'T MOVE INTO MY NEW HOUSE FOR A FEW MORE DAYS. I'M NOT HAVING MUCH LUCK COMING UP WITH GOOD IDEAS, I'M AFRAID.

IN THE AFTERNOON IT GETS REALLY HOT HERE BECAUSE THE SUN POURS THROUGH HER BIG WINDOWS.

RUFUS AND CLARENCE HUNG OUT WITH ME TODAY TOO, BUT FOR MOST OF THE DAY THEY JUST SLEPT.

7.10.94... IT WAS MY FIRST DAY OFF IN A WEEK. I THOUGHT, "AT LAST I'LL BE ABLE TO FINISH SOME COMICS."

INSTEAD I SPENT MOST OF THE DAY CATCHING UP ON MY MAIL AND TALKING ON THE PHONE...HATCHING NEW PLANS, WHEN I DON'T EVEN HAVE TIME TO GET DONE HALF OF WHAT I'M WORKING ON ALREADY.

I READ A LITTLE, AND STARED AT BLANK PAPER A LOT.

I'M HUNGRY, BUT I DON'T KNOW WHAT I WANT TO EAT.

SHIT! IT'S ONLY 11:00 AT NIGHT (7.12.94) AND I'M REALLY TIRED. HELL, I GUESS I SHOULD BE... I WORKED ALL DAY AT MY "REAL" JOB.

NOW IS SUPPOSED TO BE THE TIME FOR JOB NUMBER TWO (DRAWING COMICS) BUT (BIG SUPRISE) MY MIND IS A BLANK. FRUSTRATION...

IT SEEMS LIKE THERE'S MORE GOOD COMICS LATELY THAT ACTUALLY HAVE SOMETHING WORTHWHILE TO SAY (JUST TODAY I READ TRUE SWAMP #2 AND HUTCH OWEN'S WORKING HARD). I WANT MY COMICS TO HAVE POINTS TOO, BUT I DON'T WANT TO SOUND TOO PREACHY.

SO ANYWAY (FOR WHAT IT'S WORTH) END RACISM, DON'T EAT MEAT, END GOVERNMENT, READ BOOKS, AND THINK FOR YOURSELF, OKAY.

...AND PLEASE SHOOT ME.

HOLOCAUST

ONE OF THE MOST PATHETIC PEOPLE I'VE EVER KNOWN WAS THIS GUY NAMED JAY, WHO I WORKED WITH IN L.A.

ACTUALLY HE WAS MY SUPERVISOR WHEN I WAS WORKING IN A WAREHOUSE PULLING ELECTRONIC PARTS.

HE'D BEEN WORKING FOR THE SAME COMPANY FOR NEARLY 30 YEARS.

ALMOST EVERY DAY HE'D COME TO WORK WITH ALCOHOL ON HIS BREATH. WE KNEW THAT SOMETIMES HE'D EVEN GO DRINK DURING HIS BREAKS.

HE HAD A HUGE MISSHAPEN STOMACH FROM DRINKING SO MUCH.

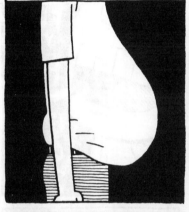

WHENEVER I SAW HIM HE WAS SMOKING. I THINK HE MUST HAVE SMOKED ATLEAST FOUR PACKS OF CIGARETTES A DAY.

AT NIGHT I'M PRETTY SURE HE JUST WENT HOME AFTER WORK AND WATCHED TV AND DRANK.

A LOT OF THE TIME AT WORK HE'D GET THE SHAKES REAL BAD.

HE WAS A SHITTY SUPER-
VISOR TOO, BUT OUR BOSSES
WOULD NEVER FIRE HIM,
EVEN THOUGH NOBODY
REALLY LIKED HIM.

ALMOST EVERY DAY HE'D
LOSE HIS TEMPER ABOUT
SOMETHING.

FUCK
YOU!
FUCK
YOU!
IT SAYS
20 NOT
21!!!

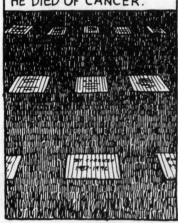

ABOUT TWO YEARS AGO
HE DIED OF CANCER.

SOME LIFE, HUH?

END.